The Mask

CJ Sparrow Publication © 2021

www.cjsparrowpublication.com

Illustrations by Rohan Daniel Eason.

Edited by Marilyn Ann Huff.

Designed by Jim Dunn.

ISBN-13: 978-0-578-569932

In memory of our beloved son.

Dirt clung to Mil's feet as he hurriedly made for the woods. It was rare to meet people along this isolated path, Mil thought. In the distance, Mil could see two children gathering wood at the edge of the forest.

Mil slowly closed the distance between them; his squat body protested in pain for his legs were bent awkwardly in different directions. Through his misshapen eyelids, he could make out a small girl and boy, bending and rising as they collected the wood. His heart leapt when he recognized the girl, Maria. She was a sweet girl, the only person who had ever cared to talk to him without cursing or ridiculing him because of his appearance.

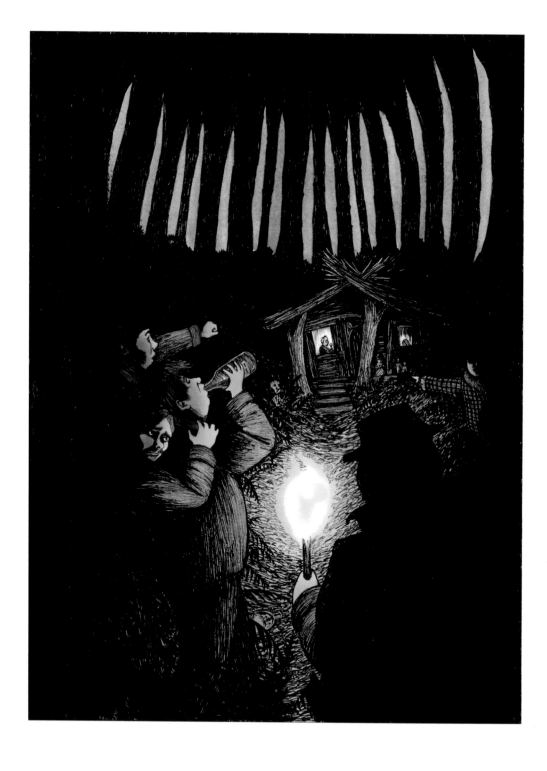

Then he saw the boy, and his heart dropped like a stone. Rufus, the cruelest boy of the village, was with her. Mil had seen him several times during the night when he and his gang soiled his house with rotten fruit and vegetables. Rufus's father was no better. On one occasion, he, along with many of the village men, came to his home and threatened to burn it down. Luckily, they were drunk and left after inflicting only minor damage to his house. The thought of waking with his house and body aflame to the cruel jeers and shouts of the villagers terrified him still. He imagined that he would have died agonizingly with his screams matching the cries of the drunken villagers.

Mil finally reached Maria and Rufus. "Hello, Maria," Mil said as he limped over towards her. "Gathering wood, I see. I hope life has been treating you and your family well."

Mil smiled uncomfortably, unsure of what Rufus would do or say. Maria opened her mouth to speak, but closed it quickly and looked away. That response, completely unexpected, hurt more than anything.

"What are you talking to her for?" demanded Rufus, his eyes narrowing. "Don't you ever speak to her again, Freak!" shouted Rufus, who then spat on him.

The spit rolled down Mil's deformed face. "You talk to this filth?" Rufus asked, turning on Maria. She lowered her eyes in embarrassment. Rufus looked at her with disgust and then at Mil with contempt. "Let's go!" Rufus barked, dragging Maria off with him as sticks spilled out of her arms. Without turning his head, Rufus called back, "My father will hear about this." Mil felt that cold terror again as he thought of Rufus's dad.

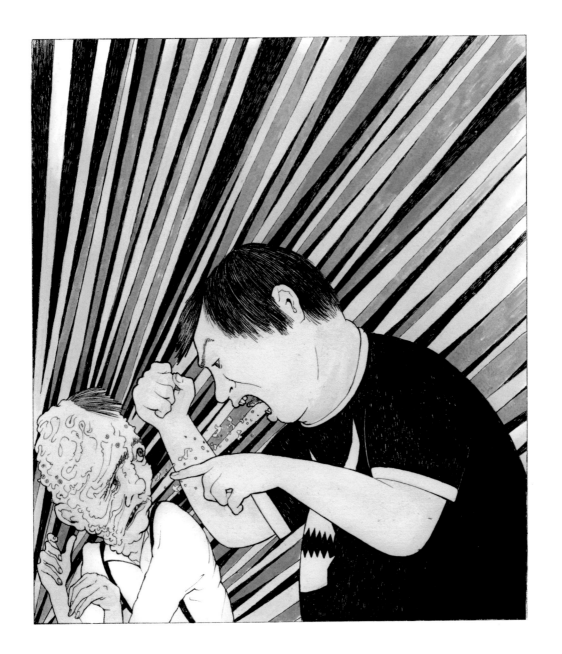

Watching Maria being pulled away, Mil felt worse than ever.

He should never have said anything. Maria would be teased and taunted at school, at the market, and at the village square. He knew that the villagers would be enraged. Mil understood why; he was referred to as the village idiot, the monster, and the freak. Mil had been born deformed and ugly, raised by his parents until he was old enough to care for himself, and then abandoned in the forest. For years now, Mil had spent most of his time collecting wood in the forest. Mil was an excellent sculptor, though the villagers wouldn't admit it.

Sometimes the people would buy his work, but it was rare since no one wanted to be near him. Sculpting occupied him in his misery and comforted him; the wooden figures that he carved for himself would not judge him as the townspeople did.

After Mil wiped the spittle from his face, he trudged through the forest in search of his special sculpting wood. Black trees loomed all around him as he made his way through the forest. Mil kept walking until something caught his eye — an object covered in dry mud stuck halfway out of the ground.

Mil looked up to the sky, which was becoming darker and darker. It was late, and he still hadn't collected his sculpting wood. But curiosity beat him, and he began to unearth the object from its resting place. As Mil scraped dirt from it, he began to see what it was. It was a bowl of some kind. No... not a bowl... a mask. Cleaning it further, Mil saw that it was pale white and made from some kind of porcelain. Mil turned it over to see the face, but he dropped it in sudden surprise. It was a plain face, but it appeared so real. It had empty, black, soulless eyes with a black sliver for a mouth, which curved in a sly smirk as if it knew everything that it needed to know. After a moment of reflection, Mil was about to toss it when the mask spoke to him.

"Toss me," it said, "and you toss away your chance for beauty." The voice was dark, and its words were spoken in a monotone.

Mil felt suddenly unclean in the presence of the mask. It was alive. There was an evil presence — something unworldly and dark, but the mask's claims had intrigued him. Mil, feeling compulsively drawn, questioned it.

He stuttered, "What...what do you mean beauty?"

"Beauty," mused the Mask. "I speak of alluring grace in the form of miraculous, physical beauty. You will turn the heads of everyone. No one will be able to resist you. Men will glare at you in envy. Women will blush and giggle as you pass and devise all manner of ways just to be in your presence if only for a moment. That kind of beauty I can grant you. Every eye of the town will be upon you." The Mask paused, looking Mil up and down slowly, and Mil felt the soulless eyes examine him. Mil heard the Mask snigger sarcastically, "I am too late. You already draw every eye upon you." Mil ignored the sarcasm. He was used to it.

"You can make me handsome?" A myriad of possibilities flooded Mil's mind. He could get married. He could have children. He could obtain a respectable job. He could even open his own business to sell his wooden sculptures. The Mask responded to his innocent question in abrupt anger.

It shrieked, "What have I been telling you? Yes! Yes! I can make you beautiful, and, yes, I am a talking mask! If you don't make up your mind and make it up soon, you can throw me back to whence I was and go to—"

Mil quickly interjected, "Okay. Okay." He did not want to lose his chance.

The Mask sighed heavily. "Before you decide, you must know this. When you put me on, we will become one — a conjoined force, if you will. You must perform a service for me when I ask it of you, and if you do not, I will die and fall away from you. You will return to your present form — a freak."

Mil nodded. "But what of the service, what am I—" The Mask cast him a dark look.

"You will know because I shall alert you when the time comes. For the rest of the time, it will be like I'm not there. Now put me on and be done with it." The Mask waited in anticipation as Mil hesitated. Something inside Mil cried against it, but he ignored it and placed the mask over his face.

It felt as if he had placed a cold blanket over his face and body. It smothered him, and he fought it, but it overpowered him. Mil could see through the Mask's slits as he circled about. He could hear laughing in his head — triumphant laughing. Mil thought he would die.

Suddenly the sensation stopped, and the Mask had dissolved into Mil's face. Fearful of the outcome, Mil touched his face apprehensively. He no longer saw out of the Mask's eyes, and as he felt his face, he could tell the difference.

"Oh my God..." he whispered. The old feeling of hardened candle wax was replaced by smooth silk. He looked at his hands. His hands! They were straight and so were his legs and feet! Mil looked down and noticed that he was taller! His spine was no longer curved, and he stood high like an elegant noble!

The Mask had kept its promise. Mil was about to run to the village, but he stopped himself. No, Mil thought. No, I will not share my happiness with them and their cruel selves. I will collect my tools and belongings and go out to another town and start a new life! They'll think I perished in the woods; they won't care. And then again, Mil stopped himself. What of Maria? Shouldn't he repay her for her kindness? So Mil, before venturing off to his new life, brought his favorite carving of Maria from his house and left it at the edge of the forest for her to find the next time she came. Then he was off, leaving his old life — forever.

Just as the Mask had described, Mil was gazed upon by all in sheer shock and wonder at such beauty. Women blushed and giggled as he strode past, waving their fans over themselves. Men stopped their talk of business; they dropped their pipes in awe. Even the children were delighted to be around him. They reminded Mil of Maria, and he was momentarily saddened to think he would never see her again, but he would not let regret stir his feelings for he had a life to live!

Mil worked as a carpenter's apprentice and soon saved enough to have his own little shop in which he could sell his beautiful wooden sculptures. And that was where Mil met Clara.

It was almost closing time when she first came to look at his work. She wasn't as attractive as the other women who came to flirt with him, but Mil knew not to judge people based on their appearances. Clara seemed more interested in his work than she did with Mil's looks, which made him even more attracted to her. They began to talk, and he learned that she also was an artist in her free time. They became close friends and soon were married. Men and women of the town were shocked that he had married someone who was far less pretty than the other women. Mil didn't care what they said or thought because he was in love with her, and she was beautiful to him. They built a place for themselves above his shop, and they worked together creating art.

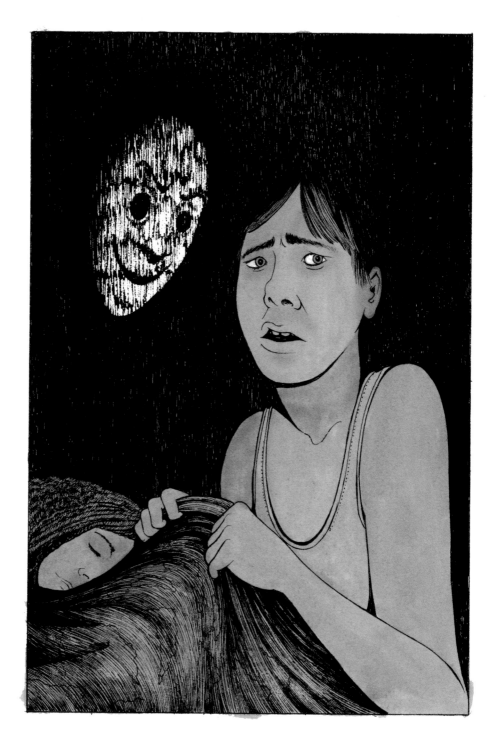

It was now, when Mil lay by his wife in bed, that he heard a frighteningly familiar voice in his head.

"It's time!" It was the Mask. "Go where you won't be seen!"

Frightened, Mil went downstairs to the back of his shop where wood shavings covered the floor and tools littered the tables. It wasn't the sudden appearance of the Mask's voice that scared him; it was the new sound of the voice. It wasn't sarcastic and dark like the first time. It sounded hungry, ravenous, as though it had been starved for a very long time. Mil had completely forgotten about the Mask. But it was here, and now it wanted him.

"What do you want from me?" asked Mil.

"You owe me a service, Mil, remember?" cackled the Mask crazily. "It has been three years since our agreement. I have done my part. You have the wonderful life you couldn't possibly have imagined. Now it is time to do what you promised."

"What am I to—" Mil began.

"Cease!" bellowed the Mask. Mil felt as though something had popped inside his head. "It will be quite easy, you being a sculptor." The Mask was practically quivering with some need that Mil didn't understand. Mil swore he could feel drips of saliva drop inside his head. "Simply find a person — any person, it does not matter who — and kill him. Once you have done this, slice the face of the person from its skull and," the Mask paused, smacking its lips, "feed it to me!"

Mil grabbed for his mouth to keep himself from retching. Mil couldn't. He couldn't take another person's life! "We made an agreement, now abide by it!" demanded the Mask. "If you do not, you will return to your ugly self and frighten away your wife and your entire new life."

"She loves—" started Mil.

"Do you really think she loves you?" scoffed the Mask. "The only reason why she is with you is because of me. Now feed me!"

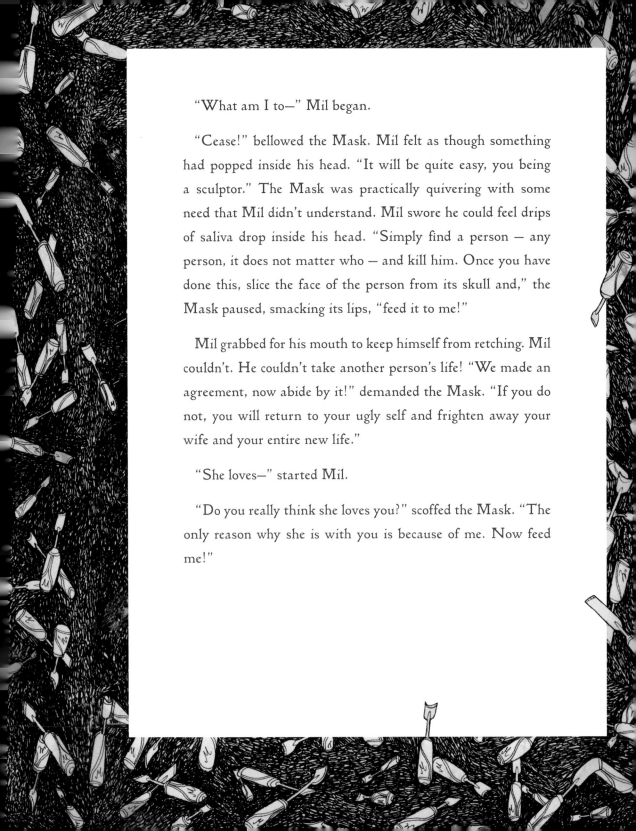

Mil let these words reverberate through his head. Mil thought of the first time he saw Clara when she walked through his shop door. He hadn't judged her then nor had he ever judged her since, and he prayed that she would do the same.

"I won't!" exclaimed Mil. "I was a fool to fall for your trickery!"

"What?!" sputtered the Mask in disbelief.

"I won't sell my soul for your looks! It's not worth it!" Mil continued. The Mask began to protest, but Mil stopped it. "Now be gone!" The Mask let out a terrible howl of defeat and rage. It was thrown from his body, the Mask shattering against the wall. Mil clung to himself as the Mask's cold darkness still lingered. Mil now looked down and felt himself. The agreement was broken. He was ugly and crippled once more, yet hope flickered in his heart.

Mil hurriedly made his way back up to his bedroom and hobbled towards his wife in bed. He didn't care what the others in the village would think or say. He only cared for how his wife would respond. She lay sound asleep, her face toward him. Mil shook Clara gently as he sat in the darkness. He quietly spoke to her. "Clara, please wake up. It's me, Mil."

Sleepily she asked, "What is it, honey?" And she opened her eyes.

Clayton Marshall Adams

Imagine a radiant smile that brightens a room or a mischievous look that says, "I could say something about that right now, but it's best I don't." Think about a sharp, incisive mind constantly searching for what's true and meaningful in life. Combine those qualities with the temperament of a poet, a writer, and a movie critic, and you have some sense of what our Clayton was like.

Clayton wrote 'The Mask' when he was 16 years old. When he shared his story with us, we did not explore with him what he was saying about his hero's world nor, for that matter, what he was saying about his own. We were simply enthralled, overcome with pride and delighted by his inspiring allegory.

School folded neatly into a myriad of other interests that Clayton pursued. His mind never stopped exploring, whether he was writing or sharing his opinions about the federal reserve system, national politics, the future of the hemp industry, or his admiration for Austrian economics. He was a very capable student. To the chagrin of his classmates, Clayton would routinely sleep at his desk in class and still managed to get high grades in his International Baccalaureate and AP classes in high school.

With courage and determination, he trained hard through various injuries for nearly three years to get a spot as a first string starter on his high school track team. Finally, in 2012, his senior year, he earned the second leg on the 4x800. And he, along with his twin brother and teammates, won first place at the Kansas City Relays, a national event that consisted of 40 schools that year.

He performed on stage as well. One evening, he surprised the family by announcing he would be performing slam poetry at the Mercury Cafe, a popular venue for writers and poets in Denver, Colorado. To conclude his spirited debut performance, with a smile, he said, "Sometimes they call me Cassius (after his hero Muhammad Ali). "And sometimes," he said with a slow, dramatic pause, head tilt, and a cocky grin, "They call me Clay." It was a triumphant night for him. The crescendo of clapping made my heart swell. The stage manager met him as he exited the stage and encouraged him to return.

Sadly, Clayton, like too many kids, was bullied at school. Vulnerable kids are singled out and targeted by bullies for irrational and senseless reasons. Clayton stood out because he was smart, sensitive, gentle, and kind. My wife and I, however, did not become aware of the extent of his bullying until a schoolmate stabbed him in the back multiple times with a pencil in Middle School. A meeting with the school's dean quickly resolved that situation but, unfortunately, this was just the beginning.

A child is often reluctant to talk about incidents that are embarrassing or situations that are shaming. Many choose to suffer, often, in silence, even when surrounded by loving friends and family. Clayton never appeared to allow the bullying to limit, defeat, or define him. What no one saw, what no one understood, was the hidden damage caused by the bullying.

Clayton's mom, an elementary school teacher, tries to help her students understand how destructive bullying is, how it can erode the fragile vulnerability of children who are just trying to fit in. She uses a heart shaped piece of paper as a metaphor to educate them how, each day, words and behavior, can crumble an individual's self-esteem, causing pain, gradually diminishing a person's spirit. What her students see, after she slowly crunches the paper heart, is a wad of paper that could be tossed into the trash. She points out that no matter how hard you try to smooth the paper out, to try to make it look like a heart again, the wrinkles and creases remain. The crumbled paper heart, she explains, represents the emotional pain and scars that can remain when people are cruel and unkind.

As a young adult, Clayton developed a major depressive disorder. It was a darkness that ultimately consumed him. He left us with so many precious memories that we cherish. This book is one of the great blessings that will endure, and we, Clayton's family, are privileged to publish it in his honor and to share it with you. After reading his story, we hope that it will inspire you to be kinder to those who are or appear "different" from you. To quote Rabbi Harold Kushner, "When you are kind to others, it not only changes you, it changes the world."

As you will discover, Clayton's story holds many challenging, unspoken questions: questions that may compel the start of conversations about the nature of love, the essence of beauty, the meaning of a committed relationship, and what it means to be human.

Thank you for this gift, dear Clayton. Rest in peace. You are forever in our hearts.

Papa, Mom, Dylan, and Evan